The Magic Hot Air Balloon

*Traveling Adventures At The Pop
Of A Bubble*

Breanna Fabian

Shannon Rooney is an unusual 7 year old, who loves bedtime, the reason being her awesome, realistic dreams start out the same way; A beautiful hot air balloon would take her to magical places every night.

After her parents would hug her goodnight and shut her bedroom door, Shannon would close her eyes and a kaleidoscope of swirling colors…

Would transform into a colorful hot air balloon. The balloon itself was clear and it was filled with rainbow colored see through bubbles instead of hot air. Inside each bubble was a tiny world. Shannon would climb into the woven basket and away she would fly. Each night Shannon would select a different bubble from the balloon. When she touched the bubble, she was instantly transported to the scene inside. Tonight, Shannon chose a peaceful beach bubble scene.

As she touched the bubble it popped and she could smell salty sea water. As she looked around the balloon landed on a beach. Shannon got out and walked on the warm sand. She could hear seabirds crying in the distance and the ocean waves lapping at the shore.

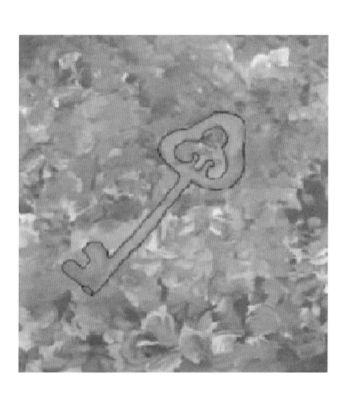

Shannon walked along the sea shore and saw something shiny. It was an old key! She bent down to pick it up, as the tide was swirling around her feet.

Then she saw a large spiral shell in the waves and picked it up. She felt a strange falling sensation as she tumbled into the shell!

Inside the shell was a spiral staircase. Shannon started to climb the slippery stairs.

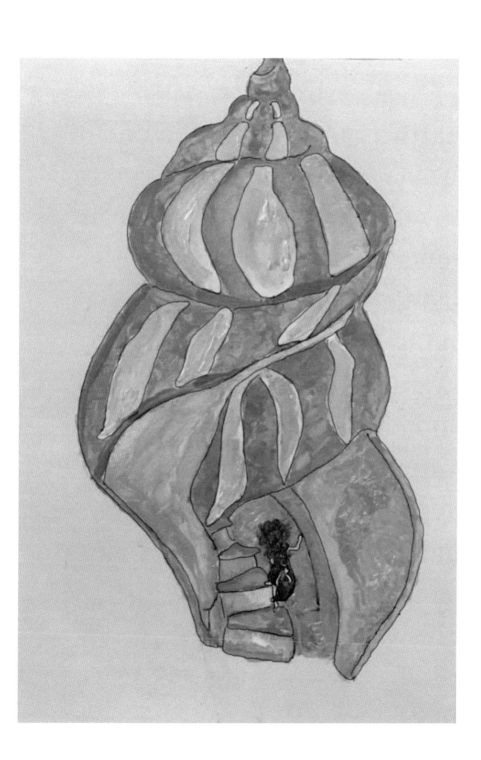

Halfway up she noticed one of the steps was missing. Looking down Shannon saw the ocean down below. Rich red corals had yellow graceful sea horses living among them. A sea turtle swam slowly by and colorful tropical fish darted through the water. Shannon carefully stepped over the missing stair and climbed to the top of the shell staircase.

There was a tiny room at the top, looking up she saw strangely illuminated windows, spiraling to the top. The only object in it was a wooden treasure chest with a golden keyhole. Shannon was so excited! She took the golden key she found on the beach and tried it in the lock. It fit! The treasure chest opened up with a squeak.

Instead of seeing gold treasure Shannon was disappointed to see something white inside. It looked like and old stuffed animal. She carefully picked it up and got the surprise of her life!

The old stuffed dog came to life! It was wagging its tail and licking her face! And even more unbelievably it was talking! He said to Shannon, "I'm so glad to meet you! My last master grew up and moved away. I have been sleeping while I waited for my new best friend to waken me.

My name is Scotty. What's yours?" Shannon was almost too surprised to answer. "Shannon" she said to him. "Do you want to come home with me?", asked Shannon, who was glad this was a dream because her parents wouldn't let her have a pet. "Let's go!" said Scotty, excitedly.

Shannon carried him down the stairs, forgetting about the missing stair in her excitement, and they slipped through…

As they fell towards the sea the balloon suddenly appears below them and Shannon and Scotty land safely in its basket.

The falling sensation must have woken Shannon up because she was now in bed again. "Wow! That was an incredible dream" she thought to herself. As she rolled over to go back to sleep Shannon felt something. She turned on the light and there was Scotty wagging away happily at her next to the bed. A knock on the door made Scotty hide under the bed. "Are you alright in there Shannon? asked her mom.

"I thought I heard something."
"I'm ok mom" Shannon
answered. "It was just a dream."
As Scotty peaked out from
under the bed, he winked at her.

"See you tomorrow night in our next adventure Scotty!" said Shannon with a yawn. And she fell asleep with a smile on her face.

Breanna Fabian is a children's book writer from Minnesota. She was inspired by very vivid dreams for this book. She enjoys making mixed media artwork and adding animations and stop motion to her pictures, she calls it "Breannimations". She also loves to play with her chinchilla Pixel and her dogs, Lucy and Sophie, shopping at the Mall of America and of course she loves to travel.

Made in the USA
Monee, IL
30 January 2022

90272688R00021